Dear Grandma

by Elizabeth Carter
illustrated by Charles Shaw

Orlando   Boston   Dallas   Chicago   San Diego

Visit *The Learning Site!*

www.harcourtschool.com

Dear Grandma,

I enjoyed your last visit very much and am looking forward to seeing you again soon. Meanwhile, I would like to carry on a correspondence with you. It would be a great way for us to keep in touch with each other. Also, I really enjoy writing letters! Do you have time to do that?

Love,
Megan

Dear Megan,

Of course I have time to correspond with you. Nothing would please me more! I enjoy writing letters, too.

I look forward to hearing about how you are doing in school, what's happening in your life, and what your favorite activities are. Our correspondence can also be a way for me to counsel you if you have any kind of problem.

Love,
Grandma

Dear Grandma,

School is fine, and so is life in general. My new baby brother is very cute. As soon as I get home from school, I like to help Mom take care of him. And you know Daisy, our dog? She's a lot of fun. I spend part of the afternoon playing with her at the park.

The only problem I have is that I'm a little behind in a project I'm doing in school. My teacher, Ms. Lopez, says I have a lot of potential but that I'm not applying myself. What does she mean?

Love,
Megan

Dear Megan,

    I have some advice to help you with the problem you are having at school. Your teacher probably means that you're spending too much time playing with the baby and the dog and not spending enough time doing your homework. Try setting aside an hour at the same time every day to do your homework. Good habits and perseverance will make it easier for you to achieve your potential.

Love,

Grandma

Dear Grandma,

Your advice really inspires me! For the past week I've been working on that project I told you about. I work for an hour or so every day, starting at 6 p.m. That way I can still play with the baby and Daisy right after school. I'm ahead of schedule now! The project is a report on someone who was able to inspire others to achieve something difficult. I chose Rosa Parks. She is such an interesting woman!

Love,

Megan

Dear Megan,

Good choice! Rosa Parks is a very important woman in American history. She is also a major figure in the civil rights movement, and I'm glad that you want to learn more about her. I look forward to reading your report myself.

Keep up the good work, and you'll soon be able to inspire people yourself!

Love,

Grandma

Dear Grandma,

Today was both a good day and a bad day. We were supposed to start giving our reports to the class today. I was the only one who was ready. I had pictures and copies of old newspaper articles to share with the class. My report was really good. The teacher said she was very proud of me, and I was proud of myself.

Something very upsetting also happened in school today. My friend, Nina, ridiculed me for trying so hard on my project. Why would she do something like that? She really hurt my feelings.

      Love,
      Megan

Dear Megan,

First of all, I am very proud of you for preparing such a good report! I know that Ms. Lopez must have been pleased. As for Nina, I think she was ashamed because she had not finished her project on time. Some people think that if they make other people feel small, then they look bigger themselves. That is probably why she ridiculed you. It sounds as if she needs someone to counsel her about what is really important.

Try not to let her comments bother you. Hold on to your sense of dignity, as Rosa Parks did.

Love,
Grandma

Dear Grandma,

    We got a new student in our class today. She's from Nigeria, and she's just beginning to learn English. Ms. Lopez wants me to be a mentor to her. She says I could help her learn English and also inspire her to be a good student. I guess that she chose me because I was the only one ready to present my report. I am proud that Ms. Lopez thinks that I am fulfilling my potential.

                            Love,
                            Megan

Dear Megan,

Your teacher has offered you a great honor. Being a mentor is a large responsibility, but it is also very rewarding. Besides, you'll be making a new friend, and you'll probably learn a lot from her, too. Please write soon to tell me more about your Nigerian friend!

Love,
Grandma

Dear Grandma,

Thanks for the advice. Batini and I have become good friends. Through her, I have learned a lot about Nigeria. I enjoy being a mentor, but I enjoy being Batini's friend even more. She's also helping me train Daisy. She loves dogs, but she couldn't have one in Nigeria. We're going to enter Daisy in a dog show next month.

Love,
Megan

Dear Megan,

    I am so glad that you and Batini have become such good friends. I look forward to meeting her sometime soon.

    I was thinking about how you and Batini are training Daisy for the dog show. Have you ever noticed the way the dogs who are in dog shows seem to carry themselves with great dignity? Daisy seems like such an energetic animal. Do you think she has the potential to remain calm during the show? You know how much she likes to play with other dogs! Let me know when the show is, and I'll try to be there!

Love,

Grandma

Dear Grandma,

Thanks for coming to the dog show. You were right about Daisy. It was pretty embarrassing when she lost all her dignity and ran to play with that other dog, wasn't it? Well, I know she has a lot of potential, so I'll try again in about six months. Maybe we should train her when there are other dogs around! Hope to see you again soon, Grandma.

Love,

Megan